Scholastic's
The Magic School Bus®
MAKES A RAINBOW
A Book About Color

SCHOLASTIC INC.
New York   Toronto   London   Auckland   Sydney

From an episode of the animated TV series
produced by Scholastic Productions, Inc.
Based on *The Magic School Bus* books
written by Joanna Cole and illustrated by Bruce Degen.

TV tie-in adaptation by George Bloom and Jocelyn Stevenson and illustrated by Carolyn Bracken.
TV script written by George Bloom and Jocelyn Stevenson.

ISBN 0-590-92251-3

12 11 10 9 8 7 6 5 4 3 2 1   7 8 9/9 0 1 2/0

Printed in the U.S.A.   24

First Scholastic printing, September 1997

Hey, Arnold, since when do you know so much about color?

Since always! Color's my favorite thing after rocks.

In Ms. Frizzle's class, a good question can lead to anything!
Take the other day, for example. We were all sitting in our classroom making rainbows.

"Why are rainbows red on the outside and violet on the inside?" Ralphie asked.

"It's because the colors of a rainbow come out according to the length of the light waves," Arnold answered. "Red is the longest wavelength and violet is the shortest."

What in the world was Arnold talking about?

"Wait until you see *my* rainbow!" Carlos said. Carlos was making a rainbow by putting different colored candy wrappers over a bunch of flashlights.

"But you need color to make a rainbow!" said Dorothy Ann, waving her paintbrush. "Not candy wrappers and flashlights!"

"But my colored candy wrappers make color by *coloring* the light," said Carlos.

"Dream on, Carlos!" said DA. "Color is color and light is light!"

"Oh, yeah? I'll show you color! Look!" said Carlos, shining a red light on Dorothy Ann's rainbow, turning it all red.

Uh-oh. This could get ugly.

Carlos! You ruined my rainbow!

Suddenly, we heard strange dings and beeps coming from inside Ms. Frizzle's closet. What was making all that noise?

"Let's check it out!" said Wanda as she headed toward the door.

"Wanda, we can't go in there!" said Arnold.

But Wanda was more curious than scared. She slowly opened the door . . . and there was Ms. Frizzle, playing on the most amazing pinball machine we'd ever seen!

"I made this machine myself," Ms. Frizzle told us. "You play by activating the Panoramic Pulse Pumper, which sends a burst of white light, better known as regular everyday light, into the machine. Then you try to make a rainbow with the white light!"

"Hold it!" Keesha shouted. "Rainbows are all different colors. How can you make a rainbow out of white light?"

"I'll be happy to show you, Keesha," Ms. Frizzle said, "but I have only one game left to do it. If I can light up all six colors of the rainbow, I get to keep the machine. But if I lose," said Ms. Frizzle sadly, "this machine will be taken away!"

We wondered who would be taking it away, but Ms. Frizzle seemed so upset, no one had the heart to ask.

You mean we have to play the game from in here?!

Yep! We've been frizzled again!

Just then, Ms. Frizzle got that funny look in her eye. "Single file, class," she said. "Time for a field trip!"

As usual, Arnold tried to get out of the trip. And much to our surprise, Ms. Frizzle said he could stay behind!

"Buckle up, class, and prepare for a colorful experience!" said Ms. Frizzle. "Take 'em away, Liz!"

But just before we took off, Ms. Frizzle got off the bus! The next thing we knew, we'd shrunk and were flying in the teeny bus toward the classroom. Then *WHOOSH*! The bus turned into a little ball of white light and flew right through the glass of the pinball machine! We couldn't believe it! We were inside the machine, surrounded by mirrors, a bunch of colorful objects, and a prism.

"I can't believe it! We're actually inside the pinball machine."

"Class under glass! Unreal!"

"How do you make the rainbow?" asked Carlos, looking at the prism and mirrors inside the game.

"By getting colored light into the colored eyes," said Ms. Frizzle, pointing to the eyes on the scoreboard. "Red light has to go into the red eye, orange light into the orange eye, yellow light into the yellow eye, green light into the green eye, blue into the blue eye, and violet into the violet eye! Six colors into six colored eyes — and you only have six chances to do it!"

To show us how the game worked, Ms. Frizzle pulled back the Panoramic Pulse Pumper. When she let go of it, a ball of white light blasted up the chute into the machine.

"Totally cool!" said Wanda.

The white light then hit a mirror at the top of the chute and bounced off into a special piece of glass called a prism. We all expected the white light to come out the other side of the prism — but it didn't. Instead, six different colors came out: red, orange, yellow, green, blue, and violet! And all six colors were coming right at us!

Duck!

We all hit the floor, and the colored lights shot right over our heads! When the lights hit the black wall behind us, they disappeared.

"Oh, no!" said Phoebe. "None of the colored lights went into the colored eyes."

Is it just me, or was the light that came up the chute white?

Ms. Frizzle used the instant-replay screen to show us what had happened.

"I see!" said Keesha. "The white light went up the chute and bounced off a mirror."

"Yes!" said Tim. "Then it went into the prism."

"And it came out as all the colors of the rainbow!" DA added.

"Then the colors must have come from the white light!" concluded Wanda.

Now we knew that to make a rainbow we had to get the colored lights that came out of the prism into the colored eyes. We were ready!

"But we only have five chances left to get six colors into six eyes," worried Phoebe.

"It seems to me you've got to keep the colored light bouncing off things until it hits the right colored eye," Arnold said.

"Since the white light bounced off the mirror," Wanda added, "maybe the colored lights will bounce, too."

"Good thinking, Wanda!" said Carlos. "We could line up a mirror to bounce the red light into the red eye!"

But just as Ms. Frizzle was about to send white light pulse number two up the chute, we heard a voice. It was Mr. Ruhle, our principal!

Ms. Frizzle sent Arnold out to keep Mr. Ruhle busy while we tried to win the game.

Ms. Frizzle? Are you in there?

"White light pulse number two coming at you!" said Ms. Frizzle. She released the Panoramic Pulse Pumper. As the white light blasted through the prism, we pushed a mirror into the path of the red light. But the red light didn't just hit the mirror. It hit the mirror, a red fruit, and then bounced into the red eye!

Next we put a mirror in what we thought was the perfect spot to bounce the orange light coming out of the prism into the orange eye. "Let 'er rip, Ms. Frizzle!" said Carlos.

"White light pulse number three up the tree!" said Ms. Frizzle, releasing the white light.

The white light came up the chute, went through the prism, and split into six colors. The orange light bounced off the mirror, just as we had planned. But instead of going into the orange eye, the orange light hit a green shamrock . . . and disappeared!

"Where did the orange light go?" yelled Wanda.

Then, to everyone's surprise, the *green* light that had come out of the prism with the orange light hit the same shamrock and didn't disappear at all. Instead, it bounced into the green eye!

"Hmmm, red light . . . red fruit . . .green light . . . green shamrock . . ." DA was thinking hard. "When we see something, say, like green," she asked Ms. Frizzle, "is it by any chance *green* because only *green* light bounces off *green* objects and into our eyes?"

Ms. Frizzle nodded and smiled.

Now we knew that light bounces off mirrors *and* off things — red light bounces off the red fruit, green light bounces off the green shamrock, yellow light bounces off the yellow banana. But we still had to get the orange, blue, yellow, and violet lights into the right colored eyes. And we only had three white light pulses left.

"We need to sink two at once or *we're* sunk!" said Carlos.

"How about orange and blue?" suggested Phoebe. "They look nice together." We all agreed. So we lined up as many orange and blue things as possible. We were going to try to bounce the orange light that came out of the prism into the orange eye and the blue light into the blue eye — at the same time.

Help!!

"White light pulse number four out the door!" said Ms. Frizzle. The white light went up the chute, hit the mirror, and bounced into the prism. As before, it came out as the six colors of the rainbow. The orange light bounced off the mirror, hit one orange, then the other orange, and bounced right into the orange eye.

"Bingo!" cried Ralphie.

At the same time, the blue light bounced off a mirror, hit the blue fish, and bounced toward Carlos and his blue sweatshirt. "Why me?" moaned Carlos as it got closer and closer and closer. At the last second he ducked! The blue light whizzed over his head, smashed into the yellow bus behind him, and disappeared.

Meanwhile, Mr. Ruhle had taken Arnold to the library to look for Ms. Frizzle. Poor Arnold tried to keep Mr. Ruhle's mind off Ms. Frizzle by reading from a book. "A blue fish is blue because it bounces only blue light, which we see when it reaches our eyes."

Just then, "Grrrrrglrrrgl!!!!" Arnold's stomach growled.

"Good thinking, Arnold!" said Mr. Ruhle. "Maybe Ms. Frizzle is in the cafeteria!"

Back inside the machine, we were all set up to bounce the yellow light into the yellow eye. We were also going to try again to bounce the blue light into the blue eye.

"White light pulse number five, ready to jive!" said Ms. Frizzle.

This time, when the blue light came out of the prism and zipped toward Carlos, he was ready for it. "No way am I ducking this time!" he said — and he didn't!

The blue light bounced off his sweatshirt and into the blue eye! At the same time, the yellow light bounced off the mirror, hit the yellow banana, hit the yellow bus, and bounced into the yellow eye!

Five colors of the rainbow into the eyes, one to go!

We did it! Yellow and blue!

The last color we had to get into an eye was violet, and we had only one white light pulse left. The pressure was on!

"Last white light in sight!" said Ms. Frizzle as she let go of the Panoramic Pulse Pumper. "It's rainbow time!"

The white light bounced into the prism and split into six colors. The violet light then hit the mirror, bounced off a bunch of purple grapes, and headed toward the yellow bus.

"Oh, no! Not the yellow bus!" cried Keesha.

"If violet hits yellow, it'll disappear!" said Carlos.

"And the game'll be over!" cried Tim.

But suddenly, DA reached into her book bag and held up a violet-colored book in front of the yellow bus. The violet light bounced off the violet book and into the violet eye!

We'd done it! We'd made the rainbow! Now Ms. Frizzle could keep her pinball machine.

"Okay, Liz," said Carlos, climbing into the bus with the others, "let's get out of here!" Liz tried and tried, but no matter what she did, she couldn't get the bus out of the pinball machine.

We're gonna be pinball kids forever!

Just then, we all heard a familiar voice from the other side of the door. Mr. Ruhle was back!

Ms. Frizzle hurried from the closet and joined Arnold and Mr. Ruhle in the classroom. "Good morning, Mr. Ruhle!" she said cheerily. Then she turned to Arnold. "Arnold, I think I left my color notes in the closet. See if you can get them out, okay?"

Arnold hurried into the closet to see what was going on.

"What's going on in there?" asked Arnold as he came into the closet.

"We can't get out!" said Carlos.

We're a living rainbow!

...n bad, oh bad, oh bad bad bad!

"You know," said Arnold, "you got in there by turning into light . . ."

"Arnold! You're a genius!" said Carlos. "We got in as light — we'll get out as light!"

Liz pressed a few buttons and turned the bus into white light. But when she tried to drive us out of the machine, the bus hit the mirror and bounced right into the prism! The next thing we knew, there were six of each of us — one in every color!

"Cool!" said Ralphie. "I can be my own basketball team!" The rest of us didn't think that was very funny.

"What are we going to do? How are we going to get out of here?" Wanda cried. Wanda was not the only one who was worried. We all wondered if there would be six of each of us — one for every color in the rainbow — forever!

Then Dorothy Ann had a really good idea. "If the prism splits white light into colors, what happens when colored light goes back through the prism the way it came in?"

We decided to give it a try. "Fasten your seat belts!" said Arnold. "I'm going to hit the flipper and flip you all backward toward the prism."

Whoaaaaaaaaaaaa!!!

Arnold flipped us back into the prism. We went in as six different colors and came out the other side as white light. It was amazing! Then Liz drove the bus up and out of the pinball machine. "Open the door, Arnold! Coming through!" yelled Carlos.

Arnold opened the closet door, and we flew into the classroom and out the open window!

When we were safely outside, the bus changed us back into our normal selves. We ran in to find Ms. Frizzle and Mr. Ruhle.

"We figured it out, Ms. Frizzle," said Carlos. "All the colors of the rainbow are hidden in ordinary light!"

"Which means white light is just filled with color!" agreed Dorothy Ann.

"Speaking of color and light," Mr. Ruhle said to Ms. Frizzle, "did you, uh . . . make the rainbow?"

"As a matter of fact, *I* didn't," said Ms. Frizzle.

"Then the pinball machine is mine, all mine!" exclaimed Mr. Ruhle.

We were very surprised to learn that it was Mr. Ruhle who would've gotten the pinball machine if we hadn't made the rainbow!

"Actually, it isn't yours," said Ms. Frizzle. "*I* didn't make the rainbow, but my class did!"

"Are you sure I can't have the machine?" Mr. Ruhle asked. He looked very disappointed.

"I'm sure," said Ms. Frizzle. "But you can come here and play it whenever you want."

"Really?" said Mr. Ruhle with a smile. "Can I play it now?"

"Absolutely!" said Ms. Frizzle. "You look as if you could use a little light entertainment!"

Letters to the Editor

Dear Editor,
There's no way you can have a light pinball machine like the one in this book. Light travels way too fast!
Yours, Speedy

Dear Speedy,
Okay, okay, so we stretched the truth a little. We had to slow down the light in our magic pinball machine so the kids could see it move.
— The Editor

Dear Editor,
I've made a rainbow with my hose, and you can see more than six colors, you know.
Sincerely, N. Digo

Dear N. Digo,
You're right. A rainbow contains all the colors from red to violet, but we showed only the six that most people see.
— The Editor

Dear Editor,
Me again. You know, you could make a pinball machine using light if you used a laser. Then at least you'd see the beams.
Yours, Speedy

Dear Speedy,
That's what we'll do next time!
— The Editor

A Note from Ms. Frizzle

Did you like my pinball machine? Pretty enLIGHTening, if I do say so myself! You know, you don't need a magic machine to play with light and color. Remember what Carlos was doing with his candy wrappers and flashlight? Transparent things (like candy wrappers and theater gels) act like gates. They let their own color of light through and block off all the other colors. Shine your flashlight onto a white wall, then put a transparent candy wrapper in front of it. What happens? What color light is it letting through? What happens when you put more than one wrapper on the flashlight at the same time? Try different combinations of colors to see what happens. It's time to take chances, make mistakes, and get color out of white light!

Ms. Frizzle